Tomie de Paola's
KITTEN KIDS™
and the Treasure Hunt

WITHDRAWN

D1531047

Katie's little brother came running. He loved it when
Katie got excited about something. It meant she was
planning an adventure.

Katie showed the cereal box to Kit. "I'll bet this map tells where a real pirate buried a real treasure!" she said. "And you and I are going to find it!"

"Uh-oh," said Kit.

Katie's ideas were fun, but some of them were a little
crazy. Like the time she found a carpet and thought it
was magic. They had to spend a whole afternoon trying
to make it fly. And the time she thought she found an
enchanted frog. She made Kit kiss it to see if it would
turn into a prince, but the frog just blinked and hopped
away.

"How do you know the map is real?" Kit asked.
"Well, look at this!" said Katie. "There's a bent old tree on the map. It's just like the one in Grandma and Grandpa's backyard!"

Kit squinted his eyes. Maybe the picture did look a teeny-tiny bit like Grandma and Grandpa's tree. "Then that's where we should start," he said.

As they ate their breakfast they thought about how much fun they would have when they found their fortune.

"We could travel all over the world!" Katie said.

"And I could ride on the back of an elephant!" said Kit.

They got their shovels and bikes and rode down the block to Grandma and Grandpa's house. Kit hurried to the front door, but Katie called to him.

"Wait, Kit! Let's find the treasure first. Then we can surprise Grandma and Grandpa."

Kit loved surprises. "Okay!" he said.

Behind the house was the old bent tree. Katie pointed to a spot near it.

"Dig here, Kit," she said. "And be sure you don't dig up the flowers."

"Aye-aye," said Kit, feeling just like a pirate. And he began digging with all his might.

Very soon Kit's shovel hit something hard. "The treasure!" he shrieked.

But it was just a bone that some dog had buried near the garden.

Katie dug, too. But the only treasure she found was a squirrel's treasure—a little pile of acorns.

Katie and Kit dug and dug, but there was no sign of the pirate's treasure.

"Maybe we'd better put some of the dirt back," said Kit. He dumped a shovelful back into a hole.

Then Katie noticed something shiny in the dirt.
"A key! It's a key!" she said. "It must be the pirate's key!"
Kit jumped up and down. "If we find out what it opens, we will find the treasure!"

The key didn't open the garage door. And it didn't
open the door to the toolshed, or the basement door. But
when they slid the key into the lock on the back door of
Grandma and Grandpa's house, it fit!

"Oh!" said Katie excitedly. "The pirate hid the treasure
right in Grandma and Grandpa's house!"

Katie and Kit pushed open the door. They could hear Grandma humming in the back room above the noise of her sewing machine. They heard Grandpa asleep in his chair even before they saw him!

"Shhh," whispered Katie.

As quietly as could be, they crept through the living room and up the stairs.

They looked in Grandma and Grandpa's room. They looked in the room they sometimes slept in. But there was no treasure.

Then they saw that the stairs to the attic were pulled down. Katie and Kit had never been in Grandma and Grandpa's attic.

"Maybe we shouldn't go up there," said Kit.

"Why not?" said Katie. "Come on."

They climbed all the way to the top and went in.

In the middle of the floor was a big trunk. The top was not locked, and Katie opened it.

Inside the trunk were beautiful beads, and scarves of silk. There were dresses that sparkled, and hats with feathers.

"Oh, Katie!" cried Kit, clapping his hands. "You were right! We found the treasure!"

Then Katie and Kit dressed up in some of the treasure.

"Grandma! Grandpa!" they called as they came running down the stairs to tell them everything that had happened.

"Why, those look just like the kinds of clothes I used to wear when I was a girl," Grandma said to Grandpa with a wink. "What a wonderful surprise!"

"So that's where I dropped the back-door key," Grandpa said, but everyone was too busy talking to hear him.

"You two look dressed for a party," said Grandma. "Let's celebrate!" And to celebrate, they all had ice cream with sprinkles on top.

Afterward, Kit and Katie put back all the dirt. Kit
even put back the bone and acorns.
"The dog and the squirrel might come looking for
them," he said.

Grandpa kept the key so no one else could ever find
the treasure. And Katie and Kit hurried home to tell
Mama and Papa about their wonderful pirate adventure.